Pour Jeanne et Maminou Meeow
S.B.

First American edition published in 2010
by Boxer Books Limited.

Distributed in the United States and Canada by
Sterling Publishing Co., Inc.
387 Park Avenue South, New York, NY 10016-8810

First published in Great Britain in 2010
by Boxer Books Limited.
www.boxerbooks.com

The illustrations were prepared using hand-painted line shapes which were digitized and assembled, then colored.
The text is set in Helvetica.

ISBN 978-1-907152-35-1

1 3 5 7 9 10 8 6 4 2

Printed in China

All of our papers are sourced from managed forests and renewable resources.

Meeow
and the pots and pans

Sebastien Braun

Boxer Books

This is Meeow.

Hello, Meeow!

Today Meeow is in the kitchen.

Meeow's friends

Woof

Moo

have come to play.

Baa

Quack

Meeow
looks in the
cupboard.

What's in the cupboard, Meeow?

Moo is curious.

Baa and Quack look inside, too.

There are lots of pots and pans.

Is Meeow going to bake a cake?

Look!

Meeow picks out a green colander and a wooden spoon.

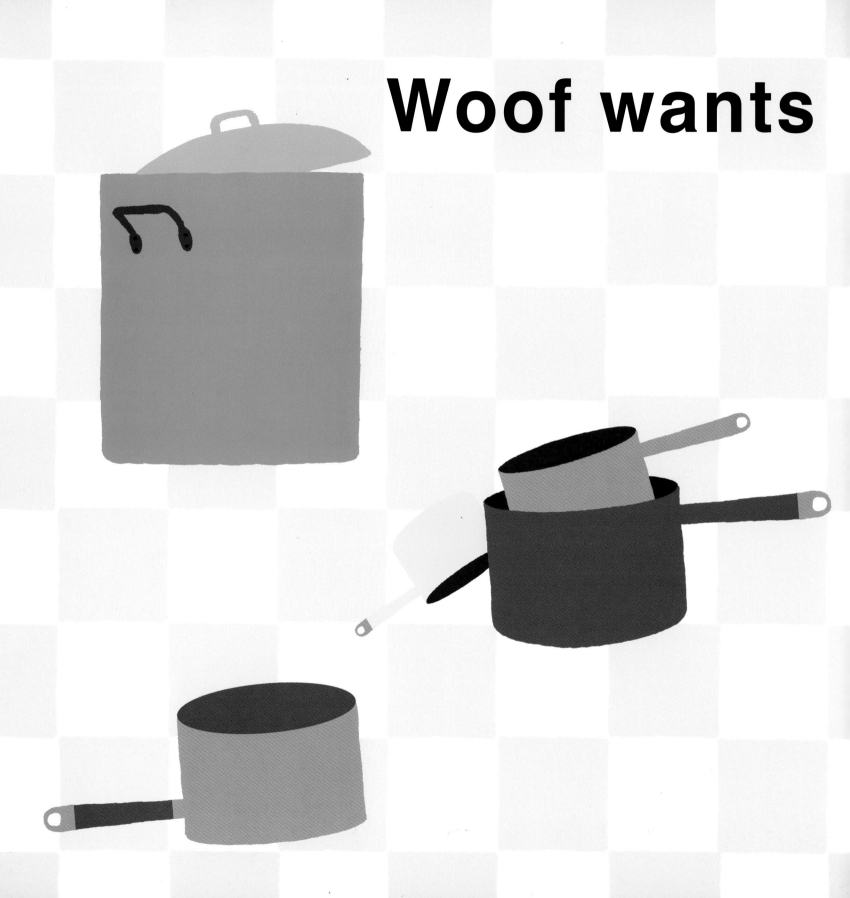

Woof wants

the orange frying pan

and the yellow fork.

Moo finds three mixing bowls—red, green, and purple. *Wobble, wobble!* Be careful, Moo!

The cupboard
is almost empty.

Baa finds two orange lids.

Good job, Baa!

Quack wears a measuring cup.

Very funny, Quack!

But what are
they going to do
with all these
cooking things?

Clang!

Rattle!

Bam!

What's all this noise?

Boom!

Boom! Clunk!

It's Meeow's band. . . .

Clever Meeow!

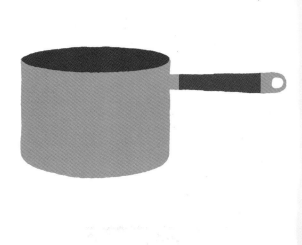